Let My People Go!

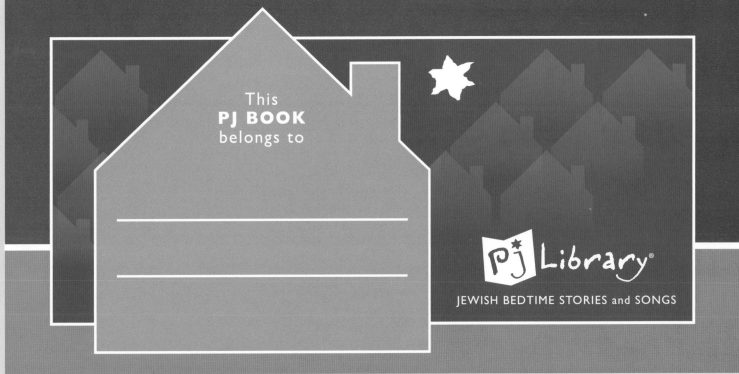

This **PJ BOOK** belongs to

_____

_____

PJ Library®

JEWISH BEDTIME STORIES and SONGS

by **Tilda Balsley**   illustrated by **Ilene Richard**

KAR-BEN
PUBLISHING

For my mother, who taught me to love reading,
and my father, who taught me to love writing. –T.B.

To my husband, Lawrence, daughter, Jodi, son, Corey,
and my dogs Bessie and Gracie I love you all! –I.R.

Kar-Ben Publishing
A division of Lerner Publishing Group, Inc.
241 First Avenue North
Minneapolis, MN 55401 U.S.A.
1-800-4KARBEN

Website address: www.karben.com

Library of Congress Cataloging-in-Publication Data

Balsley, Tilda.
  Let my people go / by Tilda Balsley ; illustrated by Ilene Richard.
     p. cm.
  Includes bibliographical references.
  ISBN 978-0-8225-7241-1 (pbk : alk. paper) 1. Exodus, The--Juvenile literature.
2. Bible stories, English—O.T. Exodus. I. Kahn, Katherine. II. Title.
  BS680.E9B35 2008
  222'.1209505—dc22   2006039740

Manufactured in Hong Kong
3 - PN - 11/1/14

031524.3K1/B0600

For more fun at your seder or in your classroom, this story may be performed as a Readers Theater script.

There are five roles.

NARRATOR- read the text in **BLACK TYPE.**

MOSES- read the text in PURPLE TYPE.

PHARAOH- read the text in RED TYPE.

EGYPTIANS- read the text in green type.

CHORUS- read the text in BLUE TYPE.

A burning bush—and it began.

As God told Moses, "Here's my plan."
But Moses was a simple man.
He said,

I just don't think I can.

POOR MOSES!

God wouldn't hear the answer, "No."
And said, "With Aaron you will go.
To lead my people from Pharaoh.
Tell him that your God said so."

So Moses spoke to mean Pharaoh,

A big mistake! He didn't know
That God would deal a mighty blow.

A PLAGUE! A PLAGUE! A PLAGUE!

Egyptians to the Pharaoh said:

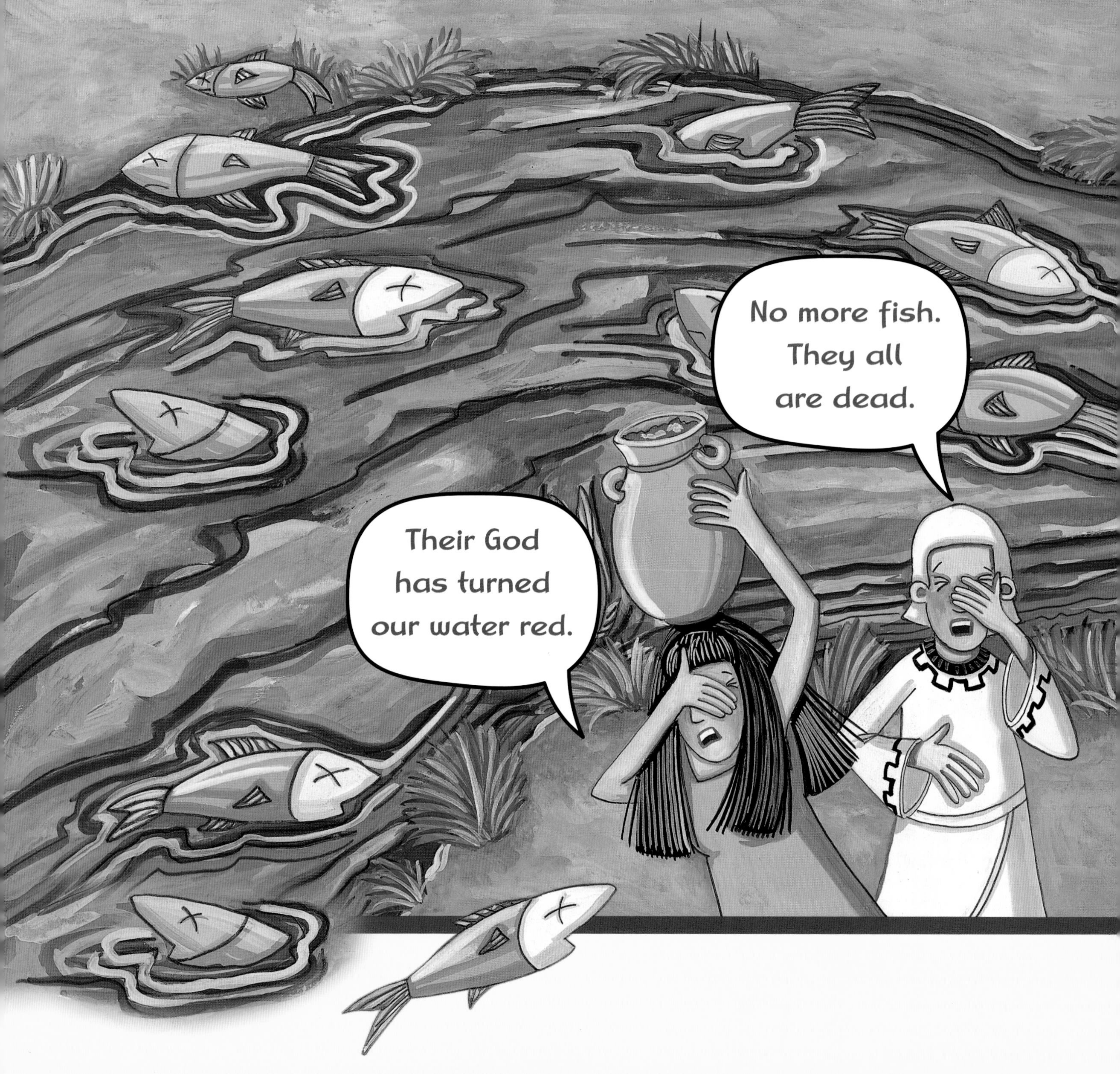

Then Moses spoke to mean Pharaoh.
"Our God says, 'Let my people go!'"
And Pharaoh shouted, "NO, NO, NO!"

A PLAGUE! A PLAGUE! A PLAGUE!

Frogs were Pharaoh's next nightmare. He cried,

> They're hopping everywhere!
> Tell God to send the frogs away,
> Then you can go without delay.
> They're in my oven, in my bed.
> I think a frog jumped on my head.

So Moses prayed, and
the frogs were dead.

Then Moses spoke to mean Pharaoh.

"Our God says, 'Let my people go!'"

And Pharaoh shouted, "NO, NO, NO!"

A PLAGUE! A PLAGUE! A PLAGUE!

Egyptians cried,
"Oh no, now gnats,
Covering cows and dogs and cats,
Covering us from head to toe,
Please, Pharaoh let those people go."

Then Moses spoke to mean Pharaoh,
"Our God says, 'Let my people go!'"
And Pharaoh shouted, "NO, NO, NO!"

A PLAGUE! A PLAGUE! A PLAGUE!

God spread the ground
with nasty flies,
But Pharaoh answered
only lies.

When Moses said, "It's done! We'll go."
Pharaoh shouted, "NO, NO, NO!"

A PLAGUE! A PLAGUE! A PLAGUE!

Soon animals began to die. Egyptians pleaded,

Hear our cry!

Then Moses spoke to mean Pharaoh,
"Our God says, 'Let my people go!'"
Pharaoh shouted, "NO, NO, NO!"

A PLAGUE! A PLAGUE! A PLAGUE!

Egyptians moaned and cried in dread.
To see their skin turn purply red
And nasty boils begin to spread.
But Pharaoh was an old hardhead!

When Moses spoke to mean Pharaoh,
"Our God says, 'Let my people go!'"
Pharaoh shouted, "NO, NO, NO!"

A Plague! A Plague! A Plague!

God continued the campaign
With hail and thunder, mighty rain.
There'd never been a worse event.
It looked like Pharaoh might relent.

When Moses spoke to mean Pharaoh,
"Our God says, 'Let my people go!'"
Pharaoh shouted, "NO, NO, NO!"

Now God sent down
a new command.
And Moses, with his
outstretched hand,
Sent hungry locusts
through the land.

A PLAGUE! A PLAGUE! A PLAGUE!

Then Egypt had three days of night
While Israelites enjoyed God's light.

A PLAGUE! A PLAGUE! A PLAGUE!

God, through Moses, said,
"Beware!
This plague is bad
beyond compare.
Death to every first-born son
From royal born to poorest one."

"But sons of Israel, I will spare.
So listen now, you must prepare."

And as God struck this final blow,
Pharaoh shouted,

"GO, GO, GO!"